THE SILENCE OF WINTER

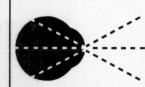

This Large Print Book carries the
Seal of Approval of N.A.V.H.

THE DISCOVERY, BOOK 2

THE SILENCE OF WINTER

A LANCASTER COUNTY SAGA

WANDA E. BRUNSTETTER

THORNDIKE PRESS

A part of Gale, Cengage Learning

GALE
CENGAGE Learning

Detroit • New York • San Francisco • New Haven, Conn • Waterville, Maine • London

GALE
CENGAGE Learning·

LIBRARY OF CONGRESS CATALOGING-IN-PUBLICATION DATA

Brunstetter, Wanda E.
    The silence of winter : a Lancaster County saga / by Wanda E. Brunstetter.
        pages ; cm. — (The discovery ; part 2 of 6) (Thorndike Press large print Christian fiction)
    ISBN 978-1-4104-5685-4 (hardcover) — ISBN 1-4104-5685-4 (hardcover) 1. Amish—Fiction. 2. Lancaster County (Pa.)—Fiction. 3. Large type books. I. Title.
PS3602.R864S54 2013
813'.6—dc23   2013004462

Published in 2013 by arrangement with Barbour Publishing, Inc.

Printed in Mexico
1 2 3 4 5 6 7 17 16 15 14 13

Blessed are they that mourn: for
they shall be comforted.

MATTHEW 5:4

CHAPTER 1

Bird-in-Hand, Pennsylvania

It was early yet, and Meredith Stoltzfus resisted coming out of the deep sleep she was in. Even though she was toasty warm under the covers, she couldn't figure out why she felt as though something was different. It wasn't the feeling of anticipation children get when they wake up on Christmas morning. It was an empty, lonely feeling.

As the cobwebs cleared, she realized it wasn't just the emptiness she felt — it was the silence and the knowledge that she was alone. Her husband, Luke, had left for Indiana yesterday afternoon, and waking up by herself gave Meredith a really odd feeling. Luke hadn't been gone twenty-four hours, and already she missed him terribly. Now she just needed to get through the rest of the days until he returned from his uncle's place, where he'd gone to learn a new trade.

After all, Meredith reminded herself, *I got through last night, and Luke will only be gone a few weeks. Now the countdown starts, and when each morning begins, it will be one day closer to Luke's return. There's plenty to do around here, so I just need to keep busy until the day he walks through our back door.*

Meredith had always been active

and very organized, and she knew these traits could be used to her advantage. It was time to fill any vulnerable moments by doing something constructive.

Rolling over onto her side and snuggling deeper under the covers, she was reminded that each morning since she'd married Luke fourteen months ago had started out the same. *If Luke was here right now, I'd be waking up with him by my side.*

Just then, Fritz, Luke's German shorthaired pointer who'd been sleeping on the floor beside the bed, snorted several times, sounding like he was snoring.

Meredith giggled, suddenly realizing what else was different this morning. She missed Luke's snoring. The small simple sound seemed to start Meredith's day out right. It was a gentle noise — not the deep rumbling her dad's snoring had always been. Dad had mentioned once that even in his younger days, he'd snored really loud. He'd blamed it on his slightly crooked nose, which had been broken when he'd run into a tree while playing ball as a boy. He said he had trouble breathing out one side of his nose — especially when he was sleeping. Meredith figured that must be true, because when Dad fell asleep in his easy chair each evening after supper, his mouth hung slightly open. When Meredith still lived at home, she'd heard the rumbling snores coming from Mom and Dad's bedroom almost every single night. Sometimes it had been so loud she'd had to cover her ears with two pillows in order to get to sleep.

Poor Mom, Meredith thought. *I don't know how she gets any sleep at all. But then, maybe Mom's not bothered by Dad's snoring. Could be she's gotten used to it over the years.*

Meredith glanced at the alarm clock on the table by her bed. Rarely did it have the chance to go off, because Luke's snoring would start within minutes of when they were supposed to get up. It was amazing that Luke never snored during the night. If he did, it must be really quiet, because Meredith had never heard it, nor had it ever caused her to wake up until the morning hours.

Lying under the covers and continuing to enjoy her thoughts, she recollected how on most mornings it was hard not to laugh at the sounds

Luke made. He sounded so content with each breath he took in and blew out, and she would just lie there quietly with her hand over her mouth and listen.

Luke didn't seem to mind when Meredith playfully tickled his ear to gently wake him up. That was quite evident when those turquoise eyes opened slowly and looked tenderly into hers. He'd often said that a tickle on the ear was far better than any blaring alarm.

Meredith's thoughts halted when Fritz, grunting loudly, woke himself up and rose to his feet. Then he plodded over to Meredith's side of the bed, nudged her arm with his wet nose, and laid his head on the mattress, watching her intently with his big brown puppy-dog eyes. When he didn't get a response, Fritz started whimpering.

"I know, I know," she said, clutching Luke's pillow tightly to her chest. "You need to go out, don't you, pup?"

Woof! Woof! The dog's tail wagged at Meredith's response.

Hearing the sound of sleet pelting the bedroom window, Meredith wished she could lie in bed a few minutes longer, hugging her husband's pillow, but with Fritz needing to go outside, any more daydreaming was out of the question. Besides, she had an appointment with a midwife. It was time to get ready for what she hoped would be some really good news.

Pittsburgh, Pennsylvania

Alex Mitchell reached into his pants pocket and pulled out the gold pocket watch he'd taken from the Amish man he'd accosted in the Philadelphia bus station. It was just a few minutes past eight o'clock, he noted. He'd transferred to yet another bus thirty minutes ago, and as they headed out of the city, the bus, along with all the other traffic, was almost at a standstill. The bus he'd ridden on after leaving the station in Philly at 12:20 that morning had been a slow-go as the foggy mist had turned to black ice on the highway. Now the roads were so icy that no one could go anywhere without sliding all over the place. Motorists had no choice but to sit and wait for the salt trucks to come through in order to make travel somewhat safer.

Alex looked out the window and saw that all the other cars on the highway had pulled off to the side of the road, just as the bus had done. According to the bus schedule, they weren't supposed to arrive in South Bend, Indiana, until 6:35 that evening, but with the weather being so bad, he figured it might be midnight or even later before they pulled into the station. Well, he didn't care. He had food in his belly, a wallet full of money, and a ticket to freedom, courtesy of the Amish man, so he'd just sit back and try to relax until the bus took him to his destination. Even Alex's nagging cough was a bit better now that he wore warm clothes and had the comfort of being on the bus.

Continuing to stare out at the nasty

weather and listen to sleet hit the bus windows, Alex was glad to be in a place that was warm. Thinking back to the night before, Alex was surprised that his luck had held out and he hadn't been caught — either by the drug dealers who'd been after him, or worse yet, the cops. He'd expected something to go wrong, because it usually did. But so far, nothing was out of the ordinary, and everything was going okay. The more distance Alex put between him and Philadelphia, the better he felt.

He looked down at the black felt hat in his lap and grinned. Luck had been with him once again, in that everything that had taken place at the bus station in Philly had happened late at night. Alex was sure that no one else had seen what had actually transpired between him and the young Amish man in the restroom. He felt pretty comfortable that the bus he'd boarded after the encounter had pulled out before anyone had discovered the unconscious man lying on the restroom floor where he'd left him. Of course, it wasn't uncommon for the bathroom in Philadelphia's bus depot to be void of activity so late at night. He ought to know — he'd slept in that depot a time or two when he'd been down on his luck. He'd never gotten used to the achiness that permeated his body each time he'd flaked out on an uncomfortable bench or awakened on a cold concrete floor. It was just one more thing that added to his unhappy life as a homeless drug addict.

I wonder if that guy had a dog like this one, Alex pondered, rubbing his thumb over the etching on the front of the Amish fellow's watch.

He stared at the picture of the bird dog engraved on the outer case of the pocket watch and clasped his fingers tightly around it. *That poor guy never knew what hit him.* Truth was, Alex didn't remember a whole lot about the beating, except that he'd gone berserk and started kicking and punching when the Amish fellow had refused to hand over his wallet. Once Alex had started his tirade, he'd been oblivious to everything around him and unable to stop himself. After he'd finally come to his senses, he'd taken the unconscious man's wallet, clothes, bus ticket, and pocket watch, then left him on the cold bathroom floor. After that, he'd rushed out the door, not knowing, or even caring, how badly the man might have been hurt.

If Alex was a decent sort, he would have gone back to make sure the guy wasn't dead. But Alex hadn't been decent for a good many years. Maybe he never had been. Maybe he'd always been full of hate. After the beating, all Alex had cared about was saving his own hide and getting out of there as fast as he could. Now if only this bus would get moving and put more miles between him and Philly, Alex would feel a whole lot better about things. What if the Amish guy had come to and told the police about the mugging? The police could be looking for him right now. Would they know he was on his way to

Indiana, dressed in the Amish man's clothes, and using his bus ticket? Alex had never been to Indiana before, but he was anxious to get there, especially now.

Alex frowned and covered his ears. Awhile ago, some kid at the back of the bus had gotten the brainy idea to do a sing-along. Most everyone had joined in, even the adults. It was bad enough when they started singing "Oh! Susanna" and "The Wheels on the Bus" with all that swish-swishing, beep-beeping, and clink-clinking. Now it was even worse. They were singing "The Ants Go Marching." Alex thought he would go crazy if he heard one more rendition of that stupid song. It seemed to go on forever.

When that song was finally over, the

kid who'd started the sing-along noticed that Alex was the only one not participating, so he got some other stupid song started about being a party pooper, and on and on it went.

Sure can't wait to get off this bus, Alex thought, twisting his body toward the window and away from the sounds of that unwanted chorus. *If I had some duct tape, I'd go back there and slap it over that kid's big mouth!*

Philadelphia, Pennsylvania

Nurse Susan Bailey had just gotten off the phone with her sister, Anne, as they finalized their plans for the evening. Anne worked at the same hospital as Susan, but Anne was a physical therapist in the rehab center, while Susan worked in the critical care unit.

Susan's morning had been busy, making rounds and tending patients. She finally found the time to take a break at eleven and couldn't believe how fast the morning had gone. She'd started her twelve-hour shift at 4:00 a.m. and had missed her early morning break, so the hunger pangs she felt now told her it was definitely past time to eat.

As Susan headed down the hall to the hospital cafeteria, she figured there wouldn't be too many people there yet, and hopefully it would be quiet. During her thirty-minute break, she planned to start a grocery list. Last night before bed, Grandma Bailey had given her a small list of things she needed from the store, as well, so all Susan had to do was add

what she wanted to her grandmother's list and stop by the store on
the way home. Buying groceries was
just a small way of showing apprecia-
tion for all that Grandma and
Grandpa had done for Susan and her
sister over the years.

When Susan opened her small
cooler, she frowned. *Sure wish I'd
thought to pack more than yogurt and
celery sticks this morning. I'll just have
to make due until I meet Anne for supper this evening, because I don't want
to buy a big lunch here and ruin my
appetite for tonight.*

Even though Susan and her sister
lived with their grandparents in
Darby, just outside Philadelphia,
their jobs kept them so busy they
didn't see each other that much.
Since they both had tonight off they'd

decided to meet at a new Mexican restaurant for dinner at six thirty. Susan looked forward to biting into a zesty taco and whatever else she decided to order.

Seeing that there were only a few people in the lunchroom, Susan took a seat at one of the tables closest to the big window where she could look out at the rock garden that had been recently established by a local Boy Scout troop. This part of the cafeteria had lightly tinted glass windows that went from floor to ceiling. No matter where you sat, you could view the scene outside. The hospital had beautiful gardens all over the grounds. Different rocks of all shapes and sizes were displayed in this one, and among them sat various statues of wildlife. A squirrel statue perched on a flat rock, and a bunny rabbit sat near the edge by the grass. A family of deer gathered at the far side of the display, and a wooden wishing well sat in the center of it all. On top of the wishing well balanced a small statue of a cardinal.

Susan smiled when a real cardinal landed near the resin one then quickly flew away. It was a lovely display, and the Scouts had done a great job, but she'd heard that it wasn't quite finished. The boys were supposed to return in the spring to plant flowers among the rocks and in the bucket of the wishing well.

A little bit of color will be the perfect touch. She had just opened her container of yogurt when she was called back to the nurse's station. "Oh, my! So much for my break," she mur-

mured, putting her hand on her stomach as it growled in protest. "Guess the grocery list will have to wait, too."

She headed back to the nurse's station, where she learned that one of the CCU nurses had taken ill and left early and a new patient who'd been badly injured would be arriving on her floor soon.

At home, Susan tended to be a bit disorganized as a means of relaxing and letting down. Here at work, however, it was a totally different story. She made sure no stone was left unturned. The patients' needs were first and foremost in all that she did, and in return, the patients loved and appreciated her. Even the doctors held Susan in high regard for the dedication she displayed on the job.

Susan wanted to make sure the room was ready, and as she quickly and skillfully did her job, she sent up a prayer on the new patient's behalf.

CHAPTER 2

Bird-in-Hand

Meredith had left the midwife's office that morning feeling like she was walking on air, despite the heavy mist and icy roads that made traveling so miserable. Her suspicions had been right — she and Luke were going to be parents. She was about to burst, wanting to share the news with her folks, as well as Luke's, but it wouldn't be right to tell them without first telling Luke. She felt like pinching herself to be sure she wasn't dreaming. In July, they would be celebrating the birth of their first baby. *Oh, what a blessing from God that will be!*

After Meredith's appointment, she'd made a few stops to pick up some groceries and other things she needed. Because of the roads, she had kept her horse, Taffy, at an even, slow pace, and so far her outing had been uneventful. She hoped when Luke called from his uncle's this evening that she could hide her excitement about the baby. She wanted to wait and tell him their great news when he came home and she could do it face-to-face.

Meredith was excited to see Luke's reaction and felt sure he'd be as happy as she was. With the prospect of his new headstone-engraving business and a baby on the way, everything seemed to be falling into place at last.

In the meantime, it would be a challenge not to tell her family when she saw them next, for she knew how excited they would all be — even her sisters and brothers, whom she felt sure would enjoy having a niece or nephew to play with and dote upon. So as soon as Luke returned and had learned the news, they'd tell both of their families together.

Before Luke left for Indiana, he'd told Meredith that he thought he'd be home by the end of January, so Meredith didn't think her pregnancy would be showing that much yet. She hoped Luke wouldn't suspect any change in her looks before she had the chance to tell him.

As Meredith guided her horse and

buggy down the driveway leading to their house, she sent up a prayer of thanks for getting her and Taffy safely home. The horse had done well on the slippery roads, but whenever a car passed her buggy, Meredith had clenched the reins so tightly that her fingers ached. It had been a good thing she'd been driving her docile mare and not Luke's horse, Socks. She shuddered to think of how hard it would have been to control the spirited gelding on the icy roads.

Even though Luke wasn't there, rounding the bend and having their house come into view was a welcome sight. It was a relief to be home again, where she could relax for the rest of the day. Not that she would do that. Meredith felt full of energy, and her mind swirled with so many plans.

There was a lot to be done before the baby came, and she could hardly wait to get started.

First things first, she thought as her stomach rumbled noisily. Meredith had been so nervous about her appointment that she hadn't eaten much for breakfast. So after putting Taffy back in the barn and unloading the buggy, she went straight to the house to make something for lunch. Now that she knew for certain she was pregnant, she'd be sure to eat regular meals. After all, she would be eating for two from now on.

Cleveland, Ohio
Alex shifted restlessly in his seat, unable to find a comfortable position. This trip was taking forever, but at least the traffic was moving again,

and that annoying singing had finally stopped. Even at a slower pace, it was better than not moving at all, like they'd been forced to do earlier that morning. Their bus driver was being cautious because now the frozen mist had turned into snow. The farther west they traveled, the heavier and deeper it seemed to be getting.

The storm had really played havoc for anyone in a moving vehicle, not to mention the road crews trying to keep the roads safe enough for travel. At this rate, Alex was almost certain the bus wouldn't make it to South Bend on time this evening. But he guessed that was okay, because he really had no place else he needed to be right now. As long as the singing from the back of the bus didn't start up again, he might be able to get some sleep. The sooner he got to Indiana, the better, but at least it didn't appear the cops were after him. That gave him a measure of peace. He sure couldn't complain, as he patted his pocket and smiled to himself, knowing he had plenty of money — more than he'd had in a long time. He could lie low in a new town, not to mention buy his next fix once he found the right dealer.

Staring out the window at the falling snow, Alex noticed that the bus was slowing down as it pulled into a parking lot. He figured this must be the lunch stop he'd heard one of the passengers mention about an hour ago, and he had to admit he was starving.

As the bus pulled in, Alex realized that, according to the sign out front, the diner had a bookstore in the basement. That seemed kind of weird, but then weirdness was everywhere these days.

When the bus came to a stop, Alex noticed the singsong kid from the back of the bus had jumped up quickly, wanting to be the first one off. *Now's my chance to get back at the little runt.*

Right before the boy ran past him, Alex stuck his foot into the aisle, just enough to make the kid trip and fall.

"Oh, sorry about that." Alex gave a halfhearted apology as the boy picked himself up. *Serves you right, you little creep. Where's your parents, anyway?*

The boy didn't seem to be too bothered by it, but he got back at Alex by saying, "You got big feet, mister."

"Oh, yeah? Well you —"

"Where you headed, sir?" the elderly man across the aisle from Alex asked as they stood to get off the bus.

Glaring at the boy one last time, Alex grimaced. The last thing he wished to do was converse with anyone else, especially now that he'd have to act Amish. But it was his own fault for bringing attention to himself.

All Alex wanted to do was get something to eat, because once the bus headed back out on the road, it might not be stopping for meals again until it arrived in South Bend. Since Alex had plenty of money for a change, he planned to order something that would stick to his ribs.

"So, where you heading?" the old

man asked again.

"I'm goin' to South Bend," Alex mumbled, followed by several wracking coughs.

"Ah, so I'm guessin' you must live in one of the Amish communities around Middlebury or Shipshewana?" The man squinted his pale blue eyes as he looked at Alex curiously.

Alex gave a brief nod and hurried off the bus, hoping the few words he'd spoken hadn't given him away. When he entered the café, he found a seat at the lunch counter and placed an order for chicken and stuffing with mashed potatoes and a cup of black coffee. He was tempted to order a beer but thought better of it since he was dressed in Amish clothes.

"Mind if I join ya?" the old man

asked, taking a seat on the stool beside Alex.

"Suit yourself; it's a free country," Alex said with a shrug. *Sure wish this guy would leave me alone. Why me, anyhow? Why doesn't he bother some other poor sucker?*

The wrinkles in the man's forehead deepened. "You know, you really don't sound like any Amish man I've ever met. Where'd you say you're from?"

"I didn't." Alex grabbed the newspaper lying beside him, hoping to put an end to this conversation.

"I'm from Mishawaka," the man said. "But I know a couple of Amish families who live in Middlebury."

Alex said nothing, just kept reading the paper.

"You goin' to Middlebury?"

Alex gritted his teeth. "I'm not sure where I'm goin' yet."

"But you said you were gettin' off the bus in South Bend. Isn't that what you said?"

Alex gave a quick nod.

"There aren't any Amish communities in South Bend, so —"

Alex was relieved when the middle-aged, slightly plump waitress came and took the old man's order. Maybe the nosy fellow would be so occupied with his food that he'd forget about asking Alex any more questions. Of course, that wouldn't happen until the waitress brought them both something to eat. In the meantime, Alex needed a break, so he hopped off his stool and headed for the restroom. He was glad when the nosy guy didn't follow.

When Alex returned to the lunch counter a short time later, the old man had moved to a booth and was slurping down a bowl of soup while leafing through a book. That was a relief!

Alex dove into the hearty meal he'd ordered and washed it down with a cup of very strong coffee. He figured it had probably been warmed over from the day before, but it didn't matter to him. The food was good, and for the first time in ages, his stomach was getting full. It felt great to have some real food in his belly for a change. Stealing bits of food here and there and sometimes gulping something down that one of the restaurants in Philly had thrown out was no way to exist. Of course, Alex hadn't done more than merely exist for too many years already. Well, that was about to change.

Grabbing the last piece of chicken and stirring it through the gravy, Alex took a quick glance around the restaurant. At the end of each table, a small bookshelf held several books.

"Would you like a refill of coffee?" the waitress asked as she took Alex's plate.

"No, I've had enough," Alex curtly answered. Then he remembered he was supposed to act Amish, which meant he should probably be a little more polite to the woman. "Uh, what's with all the books?" he questioned.

"This place started out years ago with just a few books in the cases at the end of each booth. When they saw how interested the patrons were, the store owners put shelving in the basement and started adding more books down there." The waitress smiled. "Some people just like paging through them; others want to buy them. We also do a book exchange. People can bring in a book from their home and trade it with one of ours."

That was a little more information than Alex cared to hear, but he played "Mr. Polite" and listened halfheartedly to all that she said.

In order to kill some time, after Alex paid his bill, he decided to go down in the basement to check out the bookstore for himself. As soon as he entered, the musty smell of old books hit him in the face, causing him to sneeze. He walked down each aisle of books, noticing how old some of them were. The stale odor, a combination of mildew, cigarette smoke, and mothballs, gave him the creeps, and he wondered how long these books had actually been there. Alex didn't recall if the waitress had mentioned what year they'd added the store in the basement. He did, however, recognize a few books he had read in school many years ago, so he pulled one off the shelf and flipped through the pages. Reading a page from a story he'd long forgotten until now, it unlocked unpleasant memories from his dysfunctional home and abusive father.

Back then, Alex had enjoyed reading. It had been a way to escape. Of course, whenever Alex's old man had caught him with his nose in a book, he'd made fun of Alex, saying, "Why don't you get your head outta the clouds and come back down to earth? Besides, you're too stupid to understand much about what's in them books. You'll never amount to anything, boy!"

I've had enough of this! Slamming the book shut and putting it back on the shelf, Alex hurried out of the bookstore, climbed back on the bus, and took his seat. When he spotted the nosy old man, along with several others, returning to the bus, Alex shut his eyes and pretended to be asleep. *Maybe I should have bought a book,* he thought, watching through half-opened eyes as the man took his seat across the aisle. *It might have kept my mind off my need for a fix. Oh well, it's too late for that. The best thing I can do is try to get some sleep.*

A short time later, the bus driver

took his place behind the wheel, and they were back on the road.

Alex, feeling kind of shaky, turned his head toward the window and tried to focus on the weather outside, but his eyes were getting heavy, and in no time, he really was asleep.

"Look out! We're gonna be hit!" someone shouted.

Alex jerked awake and watched in horror out the front window as a gas truck, slipping all over the icy road, swerved into their lane. A terrible crash was immediately followed by an explosion.

The bus burst into flames.

CHAPTER 3

Philadelphia

The new patient's room had been ready for almost two hours. If he didn't arrive from the ER soon, Susan would have to call her sister and tell her she'd be late for supper. Her quitting time was less than an hour from now, so hopefully it would all work out. Somehow in between her duties, she'd managed to eat the yogurt she'd packed, as well as the rest of her celery. But by the time she ate supper this evening, she'd be ravenous.

It wasn't unusual for patients to be brought up from the ER later than expected, due to other emergencies that needed tending to. And that occurred more often during the winter months, when weather-caused accidents were numerous. If the patient didn't stabilize enough to be moved or had emergency surgery, that could also delay the transfer to CCU.

Back in the patient's room, she made one final check and was glad to see that everything was in order. It was after 5:00 p.m. when she finally got the official call that the new patient was being brought up.

Susan flipped on the TV to make sure it was working and turned to their local station, hoping to hear a weather report, since she'd been hearing others talk about the storm that had hit several states. The local weather was turning nasty, too, and it was comforting to know her grandparents would be safe and warm at home in Darby, instead of out on the slippery roads.

Before clicking off the remote, a special news report broke about a horrific accident that had just happened near the border of Indiana. Although she didn't hear all the details as her own patient was brought into the room, she thought about the hospital staff in Indiana who would be tending the people involved in the accident. Susan wasn't positive, but she thought she'd heard the newscaster say it involved a bus and a tanker full of gasoline.

She sent up a prayer for the accident victims, as well as the doctors and nurses who would be treating them. Susan had learned during her ER training that if there were any survivors in an accident such as this, the medical people were going to have their hands full.

Bird-in-Hand

Wednesday evening, while waiting for Luke's call, Meredith sat in the rocker, enjoying the warmth of the fire and thinking about all she would need to do in preparation for their new little one. They had four bedrooms on the second floor, and she wanted the baby in the one closest to her and Luke's room because that would be most convenient. Maybe once Luke called, she'd ask him again about painting that room, even though he didn't know yet that it would be turned into a nursery. Better yet, maybe she would just go ahead with her plans and surprise him with it when he got home. Since he'd be making money soon, taking a little more money from their bank account to buy paint shouldn't be a problem. At least, she'd convinced herself of that. And if Meredith knew Luke as well as she thought, he'd be okay with the room getting painted once he knew about the baby.

Meredith tried to ignore the fact that Luke was late calling her. She had been to the phone shack several times this evening to see if he had left her a message, but there was none. Now that it was almost nine o'clock, she'd begun to worry and had to keep reminding herself that maybe he wasn't there yet because of bad weather. The bus had most likely been traveling right into the storm. And if that was the case, the bus would be running later than normal.

It had gotten even colder, and the mist had turned to a heavy, wet snow when Meredith decided to go out to the phone shack to check for messages again. Slipping into one of Luke's jackets and tying a woolen scarf around her head, she stepped into a pair of boots and hurried out the door. She was almost to the phone shack when Fritz started barking and pawing at the fence that enclosed his doghouse.

"Oh, no," Meredith moaned. "I'm sorry, pup; I forgot to bring you in." Quickly, she undid the latch on Fritz's dog run and swung open the gate.

Woof! Woof! Fritz raced across the yard, kicking up snow and frolicking like a puppy.

She grinned as he buried his nose in the snow and then jumped forward to do it again. Perhaps he'd caught the scent of a mouse or some other small critter that was under the snow. The dog sure did look funny each time his head came up and it was covered in the white fluffy flakes.

Meredith decided to let him explore a bit while she checked for messages. That might tire the dog out and make him more willing to settle down once she brought him into the house for the night.

Stepping into the phone shack and turning on the battery-operated lantern, Meredith pressed the button on the answering machine. Finding no messages, she decided it was time to make a call to Luke's uncle. Since no one was in his phone shack to answer the call, she left a message asking if Luke had arrived yet, and if he had, would he please call.

Shivering as she trudged back to the house, Meredith noticed that it was snowing even harder. Fritz seemed to have had enough frolicking, because he was lying by the back door, snow dripping off the end of his nose. He was probably as desperate to be inside as she.

Meredith hurried through the snow and slipped when her feet touched the icy porch step. She grabbed the railing. "Whew! That was close," she said, walking carefully to the door. "The last thing I need is to fall and get hurt — especially with Luke being gone right now."

Philadelphia

"I can't believe we finally made it here," Susan said to her sister, Anne, as they took seats in a booth at the Mexican restaurant that evening. "I'm glad you didn't mind us meeting for dinner a little later than we'd originally planned."

"No problem." Anne pushed a springy coffee-colored curl off her forehead and smiled, although her dark brown eyes revealed the depth of her fatigue. Anne was thirty — only two years older than Susan, who had celebrated her twenty-eighth birthday a few weeks ago on Christmas. But right now, the fatigue in Anne's eyes made her appear to be much older than Susan. If not for that, they could have passed for twins, having the same hair color, olive-toned skin, and straight, white teeth. Both were slender and not real tall, and the only visible difference was Anne's naturally curly hair, while Susan's was straight.

"Rough day?" Susan asked, gently touching her sister's arm.

Anne shrugged. "It wasn't really rough, just seemed to be longer than normal. And it didn't help that I stayed up later than usual last night, reading that new novel I bought a few days ago."

"It must be a good one. What's it about?" Susan asked with interest.

"It's an Amish love story, and it's making me curious about the Amish way of life. It's one of those books that once you begin reading it, you just can't put it down."

"Maybe I can read it after you're done," Susan said. "And if you're that curious about the Amish, maybe you should take a trip to Lancaster the next time you have a day off."

Anne's lips curved into a wide smile, revealing her straight pearly white teeth. "Those are both good ideas. But I think I'll wait until we have the same day off, and then maybe we can go to Lancaster together. It's been some time since we've been there, and —"

A young dark-haired waitress came to take their order.

"Hmm . . . let's see now," Susan said, studying the menu. "I'm so hungry I think I could eat nearly everything listed here." She grinned at Anne. "I'm for sure getting tacos, because that's all I've been thinking about since we talked this morning."

"I'd like a taco, too, and I'd also like a burrito with some refried beans," Anne said to the waitress.

Susan bobbed her head. "I'd like two tacos and an enchilada with plenty of cheese. Oh, and for an appetizer, we'd like some of your jalapeno poppers."

"Would you like anything to drink besides water?" the waitress asked.

"Unsweetened iced tea for me," Anne spoke up.

"Make that two," Susan said with a nod.

After the waitress left to turn in their orders, Susan and Anne nibbled on the chips and salsa that had been placed on the table, while Susan told Anne about the patient who had been brought up from the ER that evening. "The poor guy was beat up pretty bad, and I think he must be homeless," she said, slowly shaking her head. "I heard he was found in the men's restroom of the bus depot and all he was wearing was the clothes on his back, which amounted to just a dirty T-shirt and a pair of equally dirty torn jeans. Oh, and there was no identification on him at all. The ER nurse handed me the bag containing his clothes but said she thought they were basically rags and should be thrown out."

"That's so sad." Anne's forehead wrinkled. "How badly was he hurt?"

"He sustained multiple injuries to his arms, ribs, legs, neck, and especially his head. Whoever beat him must have been on a real rampage, because he was a mess." Susan added that she'd read on the man's chart that he'd had a beard, but it had been shaved off in the ER in order to stitch up a nasty cut on his chin. "And of course his head had been shaved and bandaged, as well," she said. "I wonder what he could have done to make someone mad enough to beat him up like that."

"Did he say anything to you?" Anne asked.

"No, he was unconscious, and once I had him settled into bed and had assisted the doctor with his examination, the night nurse came in and took over, since my shift had ended. Hopefully I'll find out more tomorrow." Susan sighed. "I said a little prayer for the young man, because

he certainly looked like he could use
one."

CHAPTER 4

Bird-in-Hand

For the last half hour, Meredith had been lying on the sofa, with Fritz on the floor beside her, sleeping soundly. The poor dog had played himself out, and now he was even snoring.

Meredith snickered. Watching Fritz's upper lip vibrate each time he took a breath was hilarious. The poor pup probably wouldn't be too happy if he knew she was laughing at him.

Truthfully, Meredith was tired from all the trips she'd made out to the phone shack to check for messages from Luke, so she decided if she could sleep for a little while and then go back out again, there would finally be the long-awaited message from him.

She was almost asleep when a sudden knock on the front door, followed by Fritz's loud barking, brought her to her feet.

Now who would be out on a night like this, with the snow coming down as hard as it is? Meredith wondered. *And who would be knocking on my door so late in the evening?*

When Meredith went to the door, Fritz was right there with her, still barking frantically. She opened it slowly. Sheriff Tyler stood on the porch.

"How are you doing, Fritz?" the sheriff asked, looking down at the dog. But his greeting lacked the upbeat tone it usually had whenever he was in the area and had dropped by to see Luke.

"Hush, Fritz; it's okay," Meredith said, clutching Fritz's collar. Seeing the sheriff's grim expression, her heartbeat quickened. Something must be horribly wrong. Her first thought, as she invited the sheriff in out of the cold, was of her parents. Could something have happened to them? *Oh, dear Lord, please don't let it be so.*

When Sheriff Tyler motioned for Meredith to sit down, her ears began to ring. Whatever he'd come to say, it wasn't good news. Continuing to hang on to Fritz's collar, she took a seat in the rocker, while the sheriff seated himself on the sofa across from her. Fritz had stopped barking once he'd seen that it was the sheriff, but the hair on his back stood straight up as he sat by Meredith's feet, as though waiting. Even he must have sensed that something horrible had occurred.

"What is it, Sheriff Tyler?" Meredith asked, her palms growing sweaty. "Has something happened to someone in my family?"

He gave a slow nod. "I'm afraid so, Meredith. It's Luke."

Meredith sat several seconds, staring at the crackling logs in the fireplace. Slowly, what the sheriff had said registered. "Luke left yesterday afternoon on a bus trip to South Bend, Indiana," she said. "His uncle is going to teach him how to engrave headstones."

"Yes, I know. Someone in your community mentioned it when I saw them earlier today." A pained expression crossed the sheriff's face as he explained to Meredith that the bus Luke had been riding on had gotten hit by a tanker full of gas just past the Indiana border. "There's no easy way for me to say this," he said in a sympathetic tone, "but all the bodies were completely burned in the explosion. And since Luke's name was on the passenger list, they knew he was one of those on the bus."

Meredith's body went numb. How could Luke be dead? It wasn't possible. There had to be some mistake. Luke had only left yesterday afternoon, and he was supposed to arrive in Indiana this evening. She just needed to wait for his call.

"I know this must come as a shock to you," Sheriff Tyler said, leaning forward. "And I'm very sorry for your loss."

Is this what it's like when a soldier's wife is notified that her husband's been killed in combat? Everything is normal one minute, and then, all of a sudden, it's not. Meredith's thoughts were so scattered she could barely make sense of them. "No, it's not true," she whispered, letting go of Fritz's collar and slowly shaking her head. "Luke can't be dead. He'll be calling soon, saying he's made it safely to Indiana."

The sheriff left his seat and knelt on the floor in front of Meredith. "You're in shock, Meredith, and I think you need to be with your family right now. Why don't you gather up a few things, and I'll drive you over to your folks' place to spend the night? Then I'll need to see Luke's parents and, regrettably, give them the sad news."

Meredith looked down at Fritz; the dog's head rested in her lap as though he somehow knew she needed his comfort. Tears welled in her eyes as the truth began to fully register. A sudden wave of nausea hit, and Meredith's hands went instinctively to her stomach. "Oh, Luke, I should have begged you not to go," she sobbed, bending forward so that her forehead rested on top of Fritz's head. "How can I go on living without you?"

"I can't believe how much colder it's gotten," Luann King said to her husband, Philip, as they headed toward home with Philip's horse,

Dewy, pulling their buggy. She drew her heavy shawl tightly around her neck, but the bitter winter wind seeping into the enclosure of the buggy was hard to ignore. They'd gone to pay a call on Alma Beechy, a seventy-year-old widow in their church district, and had stayed a bit longer than planned so that Philip could do a few chores for Alma.

Alma and her husband, Abe, had never had any children, and three years ago he'd developed a rare form of cancer, which took his life very quickly. As was common in most Amish communities, people began looking out for Alma. To some, she'd become like a grandmother. She loved babysitting whenever a family had a need, and a couple of times she'd even house-sat for some people's pets. Alma was a sweet, generous person, and when she had a need, someone was always there to help out. She was an excellent cook, so to show her gratitude, she would usually treat them to a delicious meal.

"You're right about the weather," Philip said after a brief pause. "The snow's coming down much harder now, too. Guess we should have left Alma's place a little sooner than we did, but I really wanted to do a few extra chores for her — especially after eating that great-tasting supper she cooked for us."

Luann smiled and patted her husband's stomach. "*Jah.* Pot roast and cooked vegetables were sure good on a cold night like this. It was nice to visit with Alma, too, but I am a bit concerned about how things are going at home."

"What do you mean?" Philip asked.

"I just hope Laurie and Kendra have everything under control and have managed to get the younger ones put to bed," Luann said. "I'm sure they didn't expect us to be gone this long."

"Those girls of ours are pretty capable. I'll bet you anything that they're gettin' along just fine. And I'm sure, if need be, your *mamm* will step in."

Luann's mother, Doris Smucker, had been living with them since Luann's father died of a heart attack two years ago, and she'd been a big help with the children. Even so, Luann had never expected her mother to do too much.

"You're probably right, but . . ."

Philip bumped Luann's arm gently with his elbow. "Sometimes I think my *fraa* worries too much about our *kinner.*"

"I know I shouldn't worry about the children, but it's hard not to when you're a *mudder,*" Luann said.

"Guess I'd better get the horse moving faster then, so we can get home quickly and you can check on things."

She shook her head vigorously. "With the way the roads look tonight, I'd rather not hurry, thank you very much." Luanne didn't normally fret when they rode in their buggy, but seeing the roads get worse by the minute had given her cause to worry.

Philip chuckled and nudged her again. "I was only kidding with you. Dewy's getting quite a workout as the

71

snow gets deeper, and he's pretty lathered up already, so I really shouldn't push him any harder. He seems to be okay going at this easy pace, though."

Dew Drop, which was their horse's real name, had been with them for seven years. He had a beautiful coat of mahogany brown and a white patch on his forehead in the shape of a dewdrop. When they'd purchased the horse from an English family who was moving out of state, one of their younger daughters, Nina, who'd been six years old at the time, had seemed quite interested as her father explained why the previous owners had given the gelding that name. Then in an excited tone, Nina had smiled up at him and said, "I think we oughta nickname our new *gaul* Dewy." The name had stuck. Dewy was a well-behaved animal and had never taken off, running out of control, like some horses did. It was as if he was born to pull a buggy, and the things that would often spook other horses didn't seem to bother him at all. It was comforting to have such an easy-going animal pulling their buggy, even if the roads were horrible.

They rode in silence for a while; then after a car went whizzing past, much too fast on the snowy road, Lu-ann turned to Philip and said, "We're so close to Meredith's house. Would you mind stopping by there before we go home? I'd like to see how she's been doing now that Luke is gone and find out if she needs anything. Oh, and with any luck, after our visit, maybe the snow will have let up, and getting us the rest of the way home will be easier on Dewy," she quickly added.

Philip grunted. "I hope you're not going to try to convince our daughter to come home with us to spend the night."

"No, no. I respect her decision to stay alone while Luke is gone. I'd just feel better if we stopped by to see how she's doing. Is that okay with you?"

He gave a slow nod. "Sure. I guess we ought to do that."

Luann smiled. Though her husband would never admit it, he was probably a bit worried about their eldest daughter, too, and wouldn't want to pass up an opportunity to visit with her. Meredith was the first of their children to leave home and get married. It had been a difficult adjustment for Luann at first, although she'd come to accept it and was glad her daughter had married such a fine man. From the beginning of Luke and Meredith's courtship, he had fit right in with her family, and since their marriage, everyone had gotten to know and like him even more.

Philip was a good husband, too, and Luann had never regretted marrying him, although her mother had expressed some doubts about their relationship in the beginning because Philip was ten years older than Luann. That had all changed, however, when Luann's mother saw how much he cared for her. Luann had to admit Philip could be a bit stubborn and opinionated at times, but he was a hard worker, devoted to his family.

The children looked up to their father, too, and usually went to him first whenever they had a problem. Even Luann's mother often sought Philip's opinion on things.

Luann just wished he didn't have to work so hard to provide for their large family. In addition to the stand he ran at the Bird-in-Hand Farmers' Market, he'd recently taken on stands at two other farmers' markets in the area in order to help with their expenses. That took up a lot of his time, so he wasn't home nearly as much as he had been before, and she and the children missed him. Feeling herself begin to relax, Luann sat quietly, watching the snow come down.

A short time later, Philip guided their horse and buggy up Luke and Meredith's driveway. When the house came into view, Luann spotted the sheriff's car parked out front.

"I wonder why Sheriff Tyler is here," Philip commented before Luann could voice the question.

"Oh, I hope nothing's wrong with Meredith." Luann clutched the folds in her dress, trying to remain patient until Philip pulled up to the hitching rail.

"Don't worry, Luann," Philip said calmly. "I'm sure the sheriff is just checking on our daughter, since he probably heard that Luke left for Indiana yesterday. News travels fast, and our sheriff, he's a good one — always checkin' on folks or just stopping by to say hello."

"I pray you're right." Luann looked toward the house as apprehension filled her senses. She had a sinking feeling that Sheriff Tyler might be there for more than just a social call.

CHAPTER 5

Meredith's heart felt like it had been torn asunder. She still couldn't believe Luke was dead, but Sheriff Tyler wouldn't have told her all of that if it wasn't true. She sniffed deeply and dried her eyes on the tissue the sheriff had just handed her, feeling dazed.

Meredith shuddered as she tried to imagine how Luke must have felt during his last moments on earth. Had he been frightened? Had he thought of her?

She swallowed against the bile rising in her throat. To be burned to death in an explosion must have been horrifying. Had Luke suffered much, or had he and the others on the bus died quickly? It was unimaginable to think that Luke had been taken from her, and in such a terrible, tragic way.

"Would you like a glass of water or something else to drink?" Sheriff Tyler asked, touching Meredith's shoulder and looking at her with concerned eyes.

"No, thanks. My throat feels so swollen, I — I don't think I could drink anything right now." And with the waves of nausea beating against Meredith's stomach, she was sure she couldn't keep anything down. Her whole body trembled, and her mind swirled with a multitude of disjointed thoughts.

"Meredith, I think we should go to your folks' house now."

Meredith remained glued to her seat as she looked past the sheriff to the corner of the room. There sat the bookcase Luke had surprised her with this past Christmas. He'd used his woodworking skills and made the beautiful oak bookcase with eight changeable shelves. Luke had mentioned to Meredith that he thought by the time they got old they'd have all the shelves full of books. Little did Meredith realize then that it would be the last Christmas she and Luke would spend together.

Her gaze went to the other side of the room, where the quilt rack Luke had given her as a wedding present sat. She'd been overwhelmed with the craftsmanship and love her husband had put into each piece of his work. It had brought tears to her eyes when he'd said that nothing was too good for his bride.

Meredith clutched the arms of the rocking chair so tightly that her fingers turned numb. There weren't many places she could look in this house and not be reminded of Luke. She'd anticipated that when he learned of her pregnancy, he would start making baby furniture right away. But that wouldn't happen now. Their firstborn would not be sleeping in a crib or rocked in a cradle that had been made by the hands of his or her daddy. Their child would never know the joy of being held in Daddy's arms, and Luke would not have the privilege of rocking his son or daughter to sleep each night.

Just then, Fritz let out a loud bark and raced into the kitchen, bringing Meredith's thoughts to a halt. A few minutes later, Mom and Dad entered the room. They'd obviously let themselves in through the back door.

"Meredith, are you all right?" Mom asked, moving quickly to stand beside the rocking chair.

"Your mamm was concerned when we saw the sheriff's car outside," Dad said, joining Mom by Meredith's side. *"Was is letz do?"* he asked.

What is wrong here? Meredith thought, unable to speak because of the lump in her throat. *Everything's wrong! How do I break the news to them when I can't comprehend it myself?*

"Meredith, was is letz do?" Dad asked again, tipping his head.

"It . . . it's Luke. He . . . he's dead."
She choked on a sob then let go of
the arms of the chair and clasped
both hands tightly against her stomach.

Sheriff Tyler gave a slow nod and
added, "I'm real sorry, Mr. and Mrs.
King, but it's true."

"Wh–what happened?" Dad asked
as Meredith rose from her seat and
sought comfort in her mother's out-
stretched arms.

Sheriff Tyler gently repeated everything he'd told Meredith about the
bus accident and ended by saying
that he needed to see Luke's parents
to tell them the sad news.

Meredith looked back at the sheriff.
"No, please. I want to tell them," she
said, swallowing hard as she leaned
heavily against Mom for support. Her

legs felt like two sticks of rubber, and her head began to pound, while the nausea increased.

"Well, you can't go alone; we'll go with you," Dad said, quickly embracing both Meredith and her mother.

Mom nodded tearfully and patted Meredith's back. "Elam and Sadie will need our support, just as you will, Daughter."

"That's fine," the sheriff agreed. "If you'd like to go there in your horse and buggy, I'll follow in my car."

"I appreciate that, but it might take us awhile," Dad said. "We shouldn't try to go very fast in this snow."

"That's okay. I don't mind going slow on a wintry night such as this," the sheriff said. "I'd just feel better following your rig and knowing you got there safely."

Fritz whined, drawing Meredith's attention to the fact that he was sitting by the front door, as though anxious to go out. "What about the pup?" she asked, still feeling as if she were in a fog.

"I'll put him in the dog run. Come on, boy." Dad opened the door, and when he stepped onto the porch, Fritz ran out behind him, bounding into the snow-covered yard.

Meredith continued to stand there, unable to think of what to do next. She felt like she was in the middle of a dream — a nightmare, really — and couldn't wake up. If only this were just a dream and she could wake from it and find everything as it had been before Luke left for Indiana. As she looked at her mother, Meredith could see the anguish hidden behind her pale blue eyes. This was not going to be easy on any of them.

As though sensing Meredith's confusion, Mom went to the utility room and returned with a heavy woolen shawl and black outer bonnet. "It's bitterly cold out tonight, so you'll need to put these on," she said, slipping the bonnet on Meredith's head and then wrapping the shawl tightly around her shoulders. It felt like years ago, when Meredith had been a little girl. Mom's motherly instinct still was to protect and comfort her.

"I know it doesn't seem like it now, but with God's help and the support of your family, you'll get through this," Mom said, leading Meredith out, while the sheriff locked the door behind them. "We all will, Daughter."

Meredith didn't see how that was

possible. With or without God's help, she couldn't imagine going through the rest of her life without Luke.

"So, what do you say, Mom, should we turn down the gaslights and head for *bett*?" Elam asked, setting his book down and looking at his wife as she smiled back at him.

Sadie set her mending aside and glanced at the clock above the fireplace. "Jah, it is getting late, so I suppose we ought to go to bed." It was almost ten o'clock, and they were usually asleep by now, but for some reason, they'd stayed up longer tonight, enjoying the quiet and each other's company.

"I'm not sure why," Sadie said, "but I have some words swimming around in my head. Maybe I'll try to make some sense of it all and write a little poem."

"It's been awhile since you wrote one," Elam said, looking at her affectionately while patting her arm. "I've always enjoyed hearing you read me the verses you come up with. I think the way you put them together in rhymes is a real talent."

Sadie smiled. It was nice to know her husband was so supportive and appreciated her desire to put her thoughts down on paper. "I guess I should keep a tablet and pen handy," she said. "Then whenever the words hit me, I can write them down."

Sadie had started writing poems when she was a teenager. It was just for fun, though, and only when the mood hit her. When she sat down and actually tried to write a poem, all the concentration in the world didn't help the words to come. It seemed to happen naturally, when she least expected it. The journal Sadie kept, with all of her writings, was worn and old, but she'd hoped one day a grandchild might take a similar interest, and she could hand down her journal to him or her.

"Think I'll take a pen and my journal to the bedroom with me and try to write a little poem before going to bed," she said.

Elam grinned. "Sounds like a good idea. Then you can read it to me like you've always done."

Just as Sadie and Elam rose from the sofa, a knock sounded on the front door.

"Now I wonder who that could be at this hour of the night," Elam said, pulling on his full gray beard before opening the door.

Sadie was surprised when Sheriff Tyler entered the house and even more surprised to see Meredith and her parents step in behind him.

"What's going on?" she asked, seeing the look of distress on all of their faces. Her hand went to her chest, and she had a sick feeling that something was horribly wrong.

"You'd better sit down," Sheriff Tyler said. "I'm sorry to say, and this won't be easy, but we've come here with some very bad news."

Sadie's knees went weak, but she couldn't sit down. Her hands started to shake as Elam's arm went around her waist for support. "Wh–what is it?" she asked. Noticing Meredith's tear-stained face, she said in a near whisper, "Is . . . is it Luke?"

Meredith nodded and burst into tears as she threw her arms around Sadie and hugged her tightly. "The bus Luke was on was hit by a tanker full of gas, and . . ." Meredith's voice faltered.

"The bus . . ." Sheriff Tyler slowly shook his head. "I'm sorry, but there were no survivors when the bus exploded."

"Oh, dear Lord, no," Sadie moaned, holding tightly to Meredith. "Not our boy, Luke! *Ach,* this can't be true!"

As Elam's shoulders began to shake, he embraced both Meredith and Sadie. Sadie's husband was usually a strong man and, with his deep faith in God, could take almost any news. But this was different. This was about their youngest son, and the loss was simply too much to bear.

The wrinkles on Elam's forehead deepened as Sadie clung tightly to him, unable to endure the tragic news they'd just received.

CHAPTER 6

The next three days went by in a blur, and Meredith didn't know how she'd made it through any of them — especially today's memorial service. Without Luke's body to view, it was that much harder to accept her husband's death. If only she could have looked at his face one last time and said goodbye. None of this made any sense, yet she had to force herself to acknowledge what had happened.

But would seeing his body really have helped? Meredith asked herself as she stared out her in-laws' kitchen window. *Would it have given me a sense of peace? No, probably not, but at least I'd have had some kind of closure.* She sniffed deeply, fighting for control as tears coursed down her cheeks. *I'm so lost without you, Luke. I don't know how I can go on.*

"Are you all right?" Meredith's mother asked, slipping an arm around Meredith's waist, while Dad, Sadie, and Elam remained at the table, murmuring words of consolation.

"I . . . I'm glad today is almost over," Meredith said, avoiding the question. She couldn't say she was all right, because it would be a lie. Truth was, she didn't think she'd ever be all right again. And Meredith knew if she'd admitted just how she was feeling right now, Mom would probably insist that she come home with them tonight so she'd have her family around her. Meredith wasn't up to that. She loved her two brothers and five sisters very much, but sometimes the younger ones were noisy and got on her nerves. She was sure that three-year-old Owen and six-year-old Katie wouldn't understand much about what had happened to Luke. And perhaps even Arlene, who was eight, wouldn't be able to grasp the agony Meredith felt. Only Laurie, Kendra, and Nina were old enough to really be supportive, but after a day of struggling to keep her emotions in check, Meredith needed some peace and quiet, and she really just wanted to be alone. Trying to be strong in front of everyone was taking its toll on her.

"Won't you come join us for a cup of coffee or tea?" Mom asked, motioning to the table.

Meredith shook her head. "No, thanks; you go ahead."

Without a word of argument, Mom gave Meredith a hug and returned to her seat at the table.

Meredith cringed as her stomach rolled. She may not have had any morning sickness before, but she'd been struggling with waves of nausea ever since she'd received the news of Luke's death. She didn't know whether it was because of her pregnancy or due to the intense grief she felt at the very core of her being.

Determined not to give in to the sick feeling, Meredith continued to stare out the window, focusing on the snow-covered yard, immersed in private thoughts. She'd been staying with Luke's folks since the news of his death, knowing they needed her support as much as she needed theirs. Dad had brought Fritz over to be with her, but even though the pup was back where he'd lived when he'd first come to be with Luke, the poor animal seemed as confused and forlorn as Meredith felt.

Fritz followed Meredith wherever she went, and on several occasions he'd actually tried to jump up in her lap. Perhaps the dog sensed her need for consolation, or maybe he'd become so clingy because he needed comforting, too. Did the pup realize that his master was never coming back?

Meredith had once read that animals could sense when their owners had died. Not long ago, she'd seen an article in the newspaper about a man's dog and how it had stood vigil every day over the grave site after its owner had passed away. She wished she could explain things to Fritz so he'd understand what had happened to Luke, but maybe he already knew. If only dogs could converse with humans, it would make it so much easier to communicate.

Meredith was thankful that everyone in their community had been supportive, bringing meals to Luke's parents and offering to run errands. They had taken Luke's death very hard — especially Sadie. Her usual cheerful smile and bouncy step had been replaced with deeper lines etching her forehead, slumped shoulders, and hazel-colored eyes that no longer held their sparkle. Her small frame had seemed to shrink.

The other day when they'd been talking about Luke, Sadie had tearfully told Meredith, "No parent ever expects to outlive their children. It's just not right."

That's true, Meredith acknowledged, swiping at another set of tears rolling down her cheeks. *And no wife expects her husband to be killed a year and two months after they're married.*

Many people — Amish and English — had come to Luke's memorial service, offering their support but not really knowing what to do or say. Luke had become a friend to many in the community. He'd exuded confidence, and even to strangers, he had seemed comfortable talking about most any subject. He'd been open minded and straightforward, and it was those qualities that people had liked about him. He'd had an infectious personality and had made many friends over the years because of it. Folks just gravitated toward him, and from the look Meredith had seen on so many faces during the service today, it was evident that Luke's death had hit the community quite hard.

Alma Beechy had hugged Meredith as soon as she'd seen her this morning. With tears in her eyes, she'd said she would be praying for Meredith during this time of need, and that if Meredith ever needed to talk, she should feel free to drop by her house, day or night.

Sheriff Tyler had come to the memorial service, too, dressed in his uniform. Meredith wondered if other places in Pennsylvania had law-enforcement officers as nice as theirs. Many times in the past when Luke and Sheriff Tyler had talked, it had been evident that the man took his job very seriously, wanting to assure a safe environment for the entire community. He was admired and respected by all the Amish who knew him. Over the years, Sheriff Tyler had developed a kinship with many people and usually took part in their community events. He was single, lived outside of Bird-in-Hand, and rarely turned down a good home-cooked meal when he was invited. Meredith remembered him saying once that even though there were plenty of good restaurants to eat at in the area, an invitation to one of the Amish homes was much better than sitting alone at a table in some crowded restaurant or having a microwave dinner in front of the TV at his home.

Sadie had written a poem about being a mother, which she'd shared with Meredith this morning before the service. It had almost been Meredith's undoing as she'd listened to Sadie read the poem in a quavering voice: "A mother wants her faith to give hope to her child; stability and trust in a world gone wild. A mother's faith should be handed down; in the next generation it will be found. A mother's faith must be steadfast and sure; so her children will desire to be like her."

Meredith smoothed the wrinkles in

her black mourning dress. She hoped she could be the kind of mother to her child that Sadie had been to Luke. He had respected his parents and been a good son to them. Meredith had never heard him say an unkind word about either one of his folks. In fact, he'd often commented on their kindness and wisdom in raising their children. He'd also said that when he and Meredith had children of their own, he hoped he'd be half as good a father as his dad was to him and his brothers.

Shifting her thoughts, Meredith was grateful that Luke's uncle Amos and his family had been able to hire a driver and come for the service — although seeing him had been a painful reminder of why Luke was dead. If he hadn't boarded that bus for

Indiana, he would still be alive, and if Amos hadn't offered to sell Luke his business, there wouldn't have been a memorial service for him today.

Amos, full of regret, had apologized to Meredith for having asked Luke to make the trip to Indiana. "I should have waited till spring when the weather was better," Amos had said with a slow shake of his head. "Sure wish I could undo the past."

Shoulda, woulda, coulda, Meredith thought with remorse. *From the very beginning, I had a bad feeling about Luke going to Indiana.* If she could go back in time, she would tell him that she was almost sure he was going to be a father. Meredith wished she could take back all the arguments they'd had after he'd lost his job. She knew just how trivial they were now. Luke having no job at all would be better than the pain of what she was going through. Now there would be no homecoming — no surprising Luke with the news of their baby. Just like that, their dreams of raising a family and growing old together had been snatched away. Luke would never know he was going to be a father, and it was too late for regrets.

Meredith hadn't told her parents or Luke's mom and dad about the baby yet. In her grief, she'd been waiting for the right time. Now that they were all together and needed something positive to look forward to, it was probably a good time to let them know.

She turned from the window and swallowed hard, trying not to break down. She'd done enough crying to fill a bathtub these last few days — especially at night in the privacy of the room she'd been given at Elam and Sadie's. "There's something you all need to know," she said, looking first at Mom and Dad and then at Sadie and Elam.

"What is it?" Sadie asked. Her face looked drawn, and her eyes appeared sunken. It was obvious that she'd done a good deal of crying over Luke's death, too, and like Meredith, she probably hadn't slept much since they'd been given the tragic news.

Meredith placed her hand against her stomach and forced a smile as tears slipped down her cheeks. "I'm expecting a *boppli.* He or she should be born sometime in July."

Mom clapped her hands, and Sadie

gasped. The men just sat with big grins on their faces.

"Praise be to the Lord; we certainly needed some good news," Sadie said, her eyes glistening with tears. "Luke's memory will live on, and we'll have the joy of knowing and loving your baby."

Philadelphia
Susan stared down at her patient, noting that there had been no change in his condition since he'd been brought to the critical care unit three days ago.

Since he had no identification, he'd been listed as a John Doe, but Susan thought that was too impersonal, so she'd decided to call him "Eddie."

"How are you doing today, Eddie?" she asked, after checking his blood pressure and other vitals.

No response. Not even an eye flutter. The poor man had been in a coma ever since he'd been admitted to the hospital, and Susan had not only been taking care of his physical needs, but she'd been praying for him often.

She thought about the day he'd been brought to her floor. When the doctor had checked the man's pupils, she'd noticed the pretty turquoise color of his eyes.

The police had come to question the patient about who'd inflicted these terrible injuries on him, but they'd been told that he was still unconscious and might never wake up. In addition to the severe trauma to his head, the young man had a crushed vocal cord, bleeding from some of his internal organs, and several broken bones, including his ribs, sternum, and collarbone. They'd been giving him medication to help dissolve the blood clot on his brain, and the patient was scheduled for surgery tomorrow.

Susan checked the man's IV and said another prayer for him. Now that he was cleaned up, he didn't look like a homeless person at all. He looked like an average young man with his head wrapped in a bandage, who needed someone to care about him.

Who are you, Eddie? Susan wondered. *Where's your family? Is anyone even looking for you?*

Bird-in-Hand
"Meredith . . . Where are you, Merrie?"
"Luke, is that you?" Meredith could

hear Luke's voice just as plain as day, but she couldn't see him anywhere. He appeared to be enveloped in some kind of a fog — yet he seemed so close to her. If she just kept going, maybe she could reach him. "Luke! Luke!" she shouted, moving forward through the haze. "Oh, please, Luke, come toward me. Let me see your handsome face."

"Meredith . . ."

"Luke . . ."

"I love you, Merrie."

"I love you, too, Luke, and I always will."

"I can't stay, Merrie. I have to go. . . ."

"No! Please stay with me, Luke. Don't go away!"

"Goodbye, Merrie. Goodbye . . ."

And then there was silence.

Drenched in sweat and clutching her bedclothes, Meredith bolted upright. Where was she? Where was Luke? Why wasn't he here beside her?

She glanced around the dark room, feeling disoriented and chilled to the bone. Slowly, she became fully awake and realized that she was in the guest room at Sadie and Elam's house, where she'd spent the last few nights. Today had been Luke's memorial service, and after she'd told Mom, Dad, Sadie, and Elam that she was pregnant, she'd come down with a pounding headache and gone to bed.

"Oh, that dream seemed so real," Meredith moaned. It was as if Luke was still alive. *Is this how it's always going to be?* she wondered. *Me, dreaming about Luke then waking up feeling the pain of losing him all over again?*

She closed her eyes, hanging on to

the last time she'd seen Luke alive. It was just before he'd climbed into his driver's car to take him to the bus station in Lancaster. She could still hear him yelling out to her as he turned and waved, "Don't worry, Merrie. It will all work out!"

Merrie. She'd always love the special nickname Luke had given her. It was short for Meredith, but he'd said he liked to call her that because she had such a joyful spirit.

It's not joyful now. Meredith placed one hand on her stomach and heaved a sigh. *If it weren't for this baby I'm carrying, I'd have no reason to live.*

Unable to endure the pain of her loss, Meredith buried her face in the pillow and sobbed.

CHAPTER 7

"Are you ready to go home, boy?" Meredith asked, turning and reaching over the front seat of Elam's buggy to pat the top of Fritz's head.

The dog whined and nuzzled her hand with his cold nose.

After spending nearly six weeks with Luke's folks, Meredith had decided it was time to go home and try to somehow get on with her life, however difficult it would be. It wasn't fair to expect Dad and her twelve-year-old brother, Stanley, to keep going over to her place every day to check on things, care for the horses, and do any other chores that might need to be done. While still in mourning over Luke's death, his mother seemed to be doing a little better now that she knew Meredith was expecting a baby, and at least she had something to look forward to, as did Meredith. So this morning during breakfast, Meredith had told Luke's parents that she would be going home, and Elam had agreed to take her. Sadie had argued at first, saying it was too soon, but Meredith assured her she would be okay on her own and would let them know if she needed anything.

I need to get back into a routine, she thought, turning to stare out the front of Elam's buggy. *There's so much to do before the baby comes, and maybe keeping busy will help me not think so much about losing Luke.*

Meredith wasn't sure how she was going to support herself. Half the money they'd had in the bank had been lost with Luke, and she'd have to be careful how she spent what was left. What she needed was a job — something she could do from her home. But what could it be?

I'll worry about that later, Meredith decided. *Right now I need to think about how I'm going to get through the rest of this day.* It wouldn't be easy going back to the house, knowing Luke would never walk through its doors again. Nor would it be easy to sit at the table and know that she and Luke would never share another meal together or take time out to discuss their day before going to bed. Everything around the house would remind Meredith of Luke. But even though difficult, she wanted to hold on to every single one of those special memories. No, Meredith's life would never be the same without Luke, but somehow, by the grace of God, she would have to learn how to deal with it. She had to — for her baby's sake.

Ronks, Pennsylvania

Luann had just entered her chiropractor's office when she noticed Sarah Miller sitting across the room, looking at a magazine. Sarah was a petite, small-boned woman in her midfifties who, except for her slightly graying brown hair, looked more youthful than some women half her age. Sarah and her husband, Raymond, had moved from Ohio to Lancaster County four months ago. Luann had heard they'd come to be near Sarah's aging parents. Raymond was a buggy maker, and his business had been doing quite well since he'd set up shop. There seemed to be a lot of buggy accidents due to all the increasing traffic, so more than one buggy maker was needed in the area. Since the Millers were in a different church district than the Kings and Stoltzfuses, Luann hadn't gotten to know them that well, but she and Sarah had spoken a few times at various community events.

"Wie geht's?" Sarah asked when Luann took a seat beside her.

Luann sighed and rubbed the back of her neck. "I'll be better once I see Dr. Warren and he works on my sore *hals.*"

"What's wrong with your neck?"

"I think I may have slept on it wrong."

"I know how painful that can be. Raymond's in with the doctor right now, getting his back adjusted."

"Did he injure it somehow?"

"No, he just woke up this morning, complaining that his back hurt. He thinks the mattress we recently bought is too hard."

"It is difficult to sleep when the bed's uncomfortable." Luann released another long sigh. "To tell you the truth, I haven't slept well since my daughter Meredith's husband died. It's been so stressful with all the worrying I've done over her. I suppose that could be another reason for my neck pain."

"Jah, stress can do all kinds of

things to a person's body." Sarah's eyes were full of compassion. "That was too bad about your son-in-law. I'd only met him once, when he'd come by the buggy shop while I was taking lunch to Raymond. I'm sure Luke's death has been hard on everyone in your family."

"It has been difficult, and try as I may, I just can't help but worry about Meredith. Even more so now that she's left her in-laws' house and has gone back to her home."

"Oh, when was that?" Sarah asked.

"Sadie left a message on our answering machine this morning, letting us know her husband had taken Meredith home soon after breakfast."

"I can understand your worry," Sarah said. "I fretted about my daughter when she lost her first husband, too. But now, thank the Lord, she's living in Arthur, Illinois, and is happily married to a wonderful man who's doing a fine job helping raise her two little ones."

"I know it's natural for a mother to worry about her children, and I'm praying that in time everything will be okay." Luann reached up to rub the back of her neck. "We do have some good news in our family, though."

"Oh, what's that?"

"Meredith's expecting a boppli in July. We're pleased about becoming grandparents, of course, and we plan to help out as much as we can, because it's going to be hard for Meredith to raise the baby alone."

"That's *wunderbaar.* Maybe after a suitable time, she'll get married again, like our daughter did." Sarah's emerald-green eyes shimmered as she smiled.

Luann slowly shook her head. "Meredith loved her husband very much, and she's taken his death quite hard, so I doubt she would ever marry again."

"But don't you suppose after some time has passed, if the right man came along, she might get married — for the sake of the boppli, if for no other reason?" Sarah asked.

Luann shrugged. "I suppose that could eventually happen, but it's hard to imagine. Right now, though, Meredith just needs her family's support."

"Of course she does. So how are Sadie and Elam doing?" Sarah questioned.

"They took the news of their son's

death very hard — especially Sadie."

Sarah's lips compressed. "That's understandable. I don't know how I could ever deal with it if something were to happen to either of my kinner. Even though our daughter lives in Illinois and her twin brother lives in Ohio, we're all very close. It was hard for Raymond and me to leave our son and move to Pennsylvania, but we knew it was the right decision once we got here and realized how much my folks needed us."

"Families needing families; that's how it should be," Luann said, fully understanding the way Sarah felt. When Luann's mother had moved in with them, even though it meant another mouth to feed, neither Luann nor Philip had seen it as a burden.

Sarah placed her magazine on the small table to her left. "Raymond and I were pleased when we received a message from our son last night, saying he'd found a buyer for the buggy shop that he and his *daed* ran together before we moved. Now that it's sold, he plans to move here, and he and Raymond will work together again." She grinned, revealing the small dimples in her cheeks. "I'm real pleased about that, and I hope it won't be long until our son finds a nice girl and decides to get married. Then our family will be complete. Since I was only able to bear two children, I'm hoping for lots of grandchildren."

Luann didn't voice her opinion, but it sounded to her like Sarah might be trying to plan her son's future, which she didn't think was a good thing at all.

Philadelphia

"How's that young man you've been caring for these past few weeks?" Susan's grandfather asked as she sat at the kitchen table with her grandparents, drinking coffee and eating some of Grandma's warm sticky buns. Anne had already left for the hospital because she had the early morning shift, but Susan wouldn't have to leave for work until afternoon.

"Unfortunately, even after several surgeries, he's pretty much the same," Susan replied, blotting her lips on a napkin. "I've been calling him Eddie, and I talk to him all the time, but he's still unresponsive."

"That's too bad," Grandma said, reaching for her cup of coffee. "Perhaps something you say will eventually get through to him."

Susan nodded. "That's what I'm hoping for, but the longer he remains in a coma, the less his chances are of coming out of it."

"Just remember, with God all things are possible," Grandpa said, placing his hand on Susan's arm.

Susan smiled. "I know that, but I appreciate the reminder." She was thankful Grandpa and Grandma had taken her and Anne into their home and cared for them after their parents had died in a car accident when Susan and Anne were thirteen and fifteen. Grandma and Grandpa were true Christians in every sense of the word, and their gentle spirits and caring actions had proved that repeatedly. Besides offering their godly influence, Grandma and Grandpa had paid for both Susan and Anne to attend college and get the training they needed to work in the medical profession. They had flatly refused to accept any rent money from Susan and her sister after they'd begun working at the hospital. Grandma had smiled and said she enjoyed having her two special girls living in their home. She'd added with a twinkle in her eyes, "You'll both be getting married someday, so you should be saving up for that."

That's not likely to happen, Susan thought. *I'm twenty-eight and have all but given up on finding the right man, and Anne says she's married to her job. I think we're both going to end up being career women — and worse yet, old maids.*

"So have you made any plans for this coming weekend?" Grandpa questioned.

Susan shook her head. "Except for going to church on Sunday, I'll probably try to get caught up on my sleep."

"What about the Valentine's banquet our church young people are having on Saturday night?" Grandma asked. "Aren't you and Anne planning to go to that?"

"I can't speak for Anne, but I'm not going."

The wrinkles in Grandma's forehead deepened. "Why not, for goodness' sake? It would be a chance to socialize with someone other than sick and hurting patients or your crotchety old grandparents."

Susan rolled her eyes. "To me, you and Grandpa aren't old, and you're anything but crotchety."

"Be that as it may, I still think you should go to the banquet," Grandma said, handing Susan the plate of sticky buns.

"No thanks, I've had my share." She patted her flat stomach. "I need to stay fit and trim so I can keep up with my patients."

"Back to the Valentine's banquet," Grandpa said, wiggling his bushy eyebrows, "you just never know who you might meet there. Could be the man of your dreams."

Susan brushed the idea aside. "I doubt that would happen. Besides, I know all the single men at our church, and none of them interests me in the least."

The three of them sat in silence for a while, until Grandma asked Susan another question.

"Do you have any plans this morning before you leave for work, or are you just going to hang around here until it's time to go to the hospital?"

"Well, I've been thinking about making an appointment at the hair salon, because I feel like I need a change."

"What are you planning to do?"

"Maybe a perm or perhaps some highlights," Susan replied. "I'm tired of my straight brown hair. Anne was the lucky one, born with naturally curly hair," she added. "She can just wash it and go, and it always looks good."

"You know me — I'm kind of old-fashioned about the idea of changing your looks on purpose," Grandma said, patting Susan's arm affectionately. "God made us all unique. I think your hair is beautiful, and it turns under so nicely when you style it." She smiled tenderly as she touched the ends of Susan's hair. "Your hair reminds me of how I used to wear mine when I was younger, before it started turning gray."

"I hope I'm as lucky as you, Grandma, when my hair turns gray." Susan smiled. "Some people are just blessed to have gorgeous gray hair, and you are definitely one of them."

"You're right about that," Grandpa agreed. "In fact, my wife is as beautiful now as the day we got married." He leaned over and kissed Grandma's cheek.

I've always hoped that someday someone will look tenderly at me, the way Grandpa and Grandma do with each other, Susan thought. *Their deep commitment to each other and the abiding love they share are so rare. To have a relationship like that is really special. But if I don't meet someone soon, I guess that's not likely to happen.*

Grandpa bumped Susan's arm gently with his elbow, pulling her thoughts aside. "If there should be any change in Eddie's condition today, when you get home tonight, be sure to let us know, okay?"

Susan nodded. She wasn't the only person who'd been praying for Eddie, and she hoped that God would answer their prayers soon.

■ ■ ■ ■

As if in some faraway fog, the man thought he heard voices. What were the people saying? Were they speaking to him?

He struggled to open his eyes but couldn't manage to pry them open. It felt as though something heavy rested on top of his head.

Where am I? Who am I? Why can't I wake up? Am I dreaming? Could I be dead?

He tried once more to open his eyes, but it was in vain.

I hurt everywhere, and I'm scared. Why won't someone tell me what's causing this pain? Will somebody please tell me my name?

The more the man fought to climb to the surface, the more the pain seemed to engulf him. It was like his body was sending out a warning, and the pain was telling him to stay right where he was, oblivious to everything else. Thinking was exhausting, and it made him hurt even more, yet he yearned for something — anything that was familiar. But it just wouldn't come.

As he fell back into his safe little cocoon, the pain seemed to go someplace else, and it was easy not to struggle anymore. He felt safe, insulated and protected in this little shell where he didn't have to think about anything at all. Slowly, as he gave up trying to figure out answers, the pain ebbed into some faraway place.

CHAPTER 8

Bird-in-Hand

Meredith put the mop away in the utility room and stopped to rub a sore spot on her lower back. She'd been home from Sadie and Elam's for nearly a week and had been working hard from the time she got up until she went to bed each night. She'd convinced herself that she needed to keep busy so she wouldn't have any spare time on her hands. Spare time gave way to too much thinking. Every night Meredith made a mental note of what she wanted to accomplish the next day. As long as she did that, she felt like she had a reason to get out of bed each morning. She realized that if she concentrated on her tasks and wore herself out, by the end of the day, when her head hit the pillow, she'd be out like a light. So far, she'd been able to do that. Pure exhaustion took over by nightfall, and she could barely stay awake long enough to fix herself something for supper.

She had put Fritz in his dog run this morning and would keep him there all day, because whenever he was in the house he always seemed to be underfoot. The other day, Meredith had nearly tripped on the dog when he'd been following her from room to room. As much as she enjoyed the pup's company, she couldn't have him inside all of the time, keeping her from getting things done. Besides, whenever Fritz approached something that had been Luke's — like his favorite chair — he would sit next to it and whine. This only made Meredith miss Luke even more.

To keep her thoughts at bay, she'd kept busy this morning, cleaning the house. The windows were spotless, and the woodwork in the living room and dining room glistened like polished stone. Meredith had cleaned it so well that the wood grain stood out, making it even more beautiful than it had been before. Luke would have been pleased with how nice it looked. Oh, if he could just be here to see it right now, the way he had been in the dream she'd had last night.

She'd dreamed that she'd had the baby, and the baby was giggling as Luke made funny noises and faces. He'd held the baby so tenderly, while looking lovingly at Meredith with his beautiful turquoise eyes. No wonder she'd awakened feeling rested for the first time since his death. It had been so real, like they'd truly been together. Meredith had actually giggled out loud in her sleep, and that's what had awakened her. If only it hadn't been a dream. Meredith had heard it said that time heals all wounds, but she didn't think any amount of time would heal the sorrow she felt over losing her husband.

Forcing her thoughts aside before she gave in to tears, Meredith gathered up the throw rugs in the living room and had just opened the door to shake them out when she heard Fritz carrying on from his kennel. Looking out into the yard, she spotted her friend Dorine's horse and buggy coming up the lane.

After Dorine secured her horse to the hitching rail by the barn, she hurried up to the house and gave Meredith a hug. "How are you doing?" she asked.

"I've been trying to get through this," Meredith answered truthfully, struggling not to cry. "I'm trying hard to be strong."

"You don't have to be strong," Dorine said with a shake of her head. "Your family and friends want to help, which is why I stopped by — to see if there's anything I can do for you or anything you might need."

"Seth came by a few days ago to

take Luke's horse out for a run, and I don't really need anything else right now." *Except for Luke. I need my husband back in my life.* Meredith couldn't trust herself to keep talking about Luke, so she asked, "Where's the rest of your family?"

"Seth is working at the Shoe and Boot store today, and Merle and Cathy are with my mamm. I had some shopping to do, so Mom offered to take the kinner for the day so it would be a little easier." Dorine leaned on the porch railing. "I love my children, but shopping with a one-year-old and a three-year-old can be a bit daunting."

Meredith nodded. When she'd been living at home before marrying Luke, she'd taken her younger siblings shopping a few times, and it had been tiring. "I appreciate you coming by, Dorine. Sometimes, with only Fritz for company, it can get kind of lonely. I do all the talking, and the poor pup just lies around looking as sad as I feel."

"I can only imagine. If animals could talk to us and share their feelings, it might help them and us to understand things better," Dorine said, glancing at her horse, who had chosen that moment to whinny. "I'm surprised you aren't still with Luke's parents," she added, looking back at Meredith. "I would think it would help to have their support."

"In some ways it did help to be there, but it was time for me to come home and get back into a routine." Meredith opened the door and motioned for Dorine to come inside.

"Let's go into the kitchen where it's warmer. We can have a cup of tea and some banana bread."

Dorine smiled. "That sounds nice."

Once Dorine had removed her shawl and outer bonnet, and they'd been seated at the table with their tea and a plate of banana bread, Meredith realized how badly she needed to take a break. She was not only tired but a bit nauseous, and the aromatic mint tea helped to settle her queasy stomach.

"This is sure good bread," Dorine said after she'd taken her first bite.

"I'm afraid I can't take the credit for it. Luke's mamm gave it to me when she dropped by yesterday."

"How's Sadie doing?"

"She's still grieving pretty hard, just as I am, but on the day of Luke's memorial service, I gave her and Elam some news and it seemed to cheer them up a bit."

"What news was that?"

"I'm expecting a boppli. It'll be born in July."

A wide smile stretched across Dorine's oval face. "Oh, Meredith, I'm so happy for you! Having the baby will not only give you some comfort, but you'll be kept plenty busy as well."

Meredith nodded. "I'm really looking forward to becoming a mudder."

Dorine took a sip of tea. "My two kinner can be a handful sometimes, but I wouldn't trade motherhood for anything. Just think, my little Merle will only be a year and half when your boppli is born. I'll bet they will become good friends once they get to know each other, just like the two of us have been for so many years."

Meredith sat silently, staring into her cup, giving no acknowledgment of what her friend had just said.

"Is there something bothering you that you'd like to talk about?" Dorine asked, gently touching Meredith's arm.

Meredith sighed deeply. "There isn't a lot left in my savings account, and I need to find something to do soon that will bring in some money before taxes come due in April."

Dorine's eyes brightened. "Why don't you make women's head coverings to sell? After all, you've been making your own since we were teenagers, and you do such a good job. A lot of women don't like to make their own coverings because it's such tedious sewing, so I'm sure you'd get plenty of orders."

Meredith pondered her friend's suggestion. "Hmm . . . I might just give that a try. It probably won't bring in a lot of money, but at least it would be something to help out until the boppli comes and I'm able to look for a full-time job."

"You're right, and once you are ready to get started sewing, I'll help spread the word."

"*Danki*, I appreciate that."

Their conversation turned to the weather then and how they couldn't wait for winter to be over so they could begin planting their gardens.

"With the boppli coming in the middle of summer, I may not get as much gardening done this year as I would like," Meredith said, taking her empty cup to the sink.

"I'd be happy to come over and help out anytime you like. I'm sure my mamm would watch my little ones for me."

Meredith smiled. "Working in the garden will be a lot more fun if we can do it together." She appreciated having such a good friend.

"Changing the subject," Dorine said, "when Seth was at the buggy shop last week getting new wheels for his rig, Raymond Miller mentioned that his son, Jonah, would be moving here from Sugarcreek, Ohio, and will be working in the buggy shop with him. You don't suppose it could be the same Jonah Miller you met in Sarasota when you worked there as a teenager one summer?"

Meredith touched her cheeks. "Oh,

my, I haven't seen Jonah in such a long time; I'd almost forgotten that he lived in Sugarcreek."

"So you think it's him, then?"

"Jah, I sure do. In the last letter I received from Jonah, before Luke and I got married, he said he was working for his daed in his buggy shop. Until now, though, I hadn't even thought that Jonah could be Raymond and Sarah Miller's son."

"I wonder if he's married, with a family of his own," Dorine said, finishing the last of her tea.

Meredith shrugged. "I don't know. Like I said, I haven't heard from Jonah in a long while, and since I didn't know Raymond and Sarah Miller were his folks, I wouldn't have thought to ask."

"I guess we'll know soon enough,

because from what I heard, Jonah was supposed to have arrived at his folks' place sometime yesterday." Dorine pushed her chair away from the table. "As nice as this has been, I really should head out now and get my shopping done before it starts snowing again." She gave Meredith a hug. "Be sure to let us know if there's anything either Seth or I can do for you."

Meredith nodded. "Jah, I will."

Jonah Miller removed the last of his clothes from his suitcase and put them away in the closet; then he placed the suitcase on the floor at the back of the closet. It was good to be unpacked. It was even better to be here now with his folks. He'd had no problem pulling up stakes and moving to Pennsylvania to partner with Dad. After all, it was just him, so making the move was a lot easier than if he had a wife and children to consider. It would be great working alongside Dad again — just like he'd done since he was a teenager, when Dad first taught him how to make and repair Amish and other types of buggies. Jonah and his dad not only had a close father-son relationship, but they were linked in a working relationship, too, and both took their work seriously. From what Dad had said, his business was growing here in Lancaster County, so Jonah figured with the two of them working together they could get a lot more done and make a good living.

For now, Jonah would live with his folks, but someday he planned to have a home of his own. He would need that if he ever found the right woman and decided to get married. He sure couldn't stay living with Mom and Dad forever, and he didn't wish to remain single indefinitely.

Jonah glanced around the bedroom he'd chosen. Just like their home in Ohio, all the rooms in Mom and Dad's new house felt homey. Maybe he'd be lucky enough to find a wife some day and have the same type of relationship that his folks had with each other. He dreamed of a spouse who would fill their home with love — a place where Jonah knew he belonged as soon as he walked through the door. His mom had a way of putting her heart into every room in her house, and anyone entering could actually feel the welcome.

Even though this new home looked pretty good, he had seen a few things that ought to be done and was anxious to help Dad, not just at the buggy shop but with some of the jobs that needed to be completed here at the house.

While Jonah and his folks had been eating supper last night, he'd learned that Meredith Stoltzfus had lost her husband in a tragic accident and that she was expecting a baby. It didn't take Jonah long to realize this was the same young woman he used to know. He was stunned by the news of her sad loss, and his heart went out to her. So today, he planned to visit Meredith and offer his condolences. He hoped this would be a good time for him to drop by, because he wanted to let Meredith know how bad he felt about her situation and see if there was anything he could do to help out. After all, they'd been close friends a long time ago.

Ever since Jonah was a boy, he'd been sensitive to others, especially when they needed help in any way. He'd had an experience long ago that had embedded kindness into his soul and actually changed his attitude about people and life. Because of that, he'd helped his twin sister, Jean, as much as he could when she'd lost her first husband. Maybe he could help Meredith, as well.

Jonah thought about the friendship he and Meredith had developed when they'd worked at a restaurant in the small community of Pinecraft, in Sarasota, Florida. Meredith had been seventeen then, and he'd been eighteen. They'd quickly become friends and after returning to their homes, had stayed in touch through letters, until Meredith wrote and said she was being courted by Luke Stoltzfus and that they were planning to be married. Jonah had been disappointed at first but consoled himself with the thought that Meredith deserved to be happy. He'd been hoping she might be the girl for him but had learned to accept it as God's will when she'd fallen in love with someone else.

Meredith was slowly bringing some normalcy back into her life. At least, she was trying. She was most anxious to get things ready for the baby, which would probably keep her busy until the birth. She looked forward to her family coming over for supper this evening. It would be nice to take a break and spend time visiting with her parents and siblings — not to mention having someone to cook for other than herself. Grandma Smucker was coming, too, so they'd all be together like it had been before she and Luke got married.

Meredith was anxious to tell her family about her plan to start making head coverings. Except for the short time Dorine had been there, Meredith had been busy working around the house all morning and into the afternoon. As soon as the weather warmed, she planned to till the garden and uncover her flower beds. She would find a place to plant the bulbs Mom said she had for her. Several daffodils and tulips would add some color to her flower beds. She would also need to trim all the shrubs around the house, the way Dad had taught her to do several years ago, when she would walk around the yard helping him with spring cleanup. Those memories were probably why, to this day, she enjoyed working in the yard and around the house.

Thankfully she'd had no problems with her house except for a piece of siding that had blown off during one of the recent windy, snowy days. Dad said he would take care of that for her when they came over this evening.

Meredith planned to fix a big pot of sloppy joes for the meal, and she'd made a macaroni salad as well as a potato salad to go with it. Mom was bringing a chocolate cake — Dad's favorite — and Grandma was bringing some of Meredith's favorite ginger cookies.

Earlier, Meredith had browned the ground beef and sautéed the onions and green peppers, so all that was needed was to add the brown sugar, salt, pepper, a little mustard, ketchup, and a jar of mild chili sauce. She'd decided to prepare that in an hour or so, giving it plenty of time to simmer before supper. Until then, she thought she'd at least get a start on painting the baby's room.

She had to get the ladder from the barn and carry it upstairs, and in hindsight, she wished she had asked Dad to help her with that the last time he was here.

Well, it was only this one project, and she had consoled herself with the fact that she would get some exercise carrying the ladder up those steps. It was still early in her pregnancy, and she wasn't even showing yet, so it would be easier to do these things now, rather than when she was big and clumsy.

Meredith took her time carrying the ladder from the barn and across the yard. She had to put the ladder down a few times — first to close the barn door, and then again when she was on the porch, so she could open the back door and get the ladder inside.

"I could sure use an extra pair of hands right now," she muttered, dragging the ladder into the house.

Next was the chore of getting the ladder up the stairs, and while maneuvering it, a sharp pain streaked across her middle just as she reached the top step. It startled her, and she had to stop for a minute and catch her breath. Meredith leaned against the wall, holding her stomach until the spasm finally subsided. Slowly, she made her way to the spare room and carefully set the ladder in the corner where she wanted to begin painting.

Standing back, she tried to visualize how the room would look once it had a new coat of paint on the walls and ceiling. Meredith knew the now-drab room would transform after the color had been changed. She couldn't wait to get started.

It wasn't a real big room, so Meredith was sure she could tackle the project herself. She'd decided on a light tan color, which would be good for either a boy or a girl. And since this room was right next to Meredith's, it would be convenient for her to check on the baby.

While thinking about putting the baby's crib in her room for the first couple of weeks, she bent down to open the can of paint she'd purchased at the hardware store the day before. She'd just gotten the lid pried loose when another pain shot through her stomach. Deciding that the painting could wait for now and realizing that she was in need of a break, she headed back downstairs.

Guess I overdid it carrying that heavy ladder in by myself, she silently scolded herself.

Before sitting down to rest, she went to the kitchen and made some tea. Then she got out the kettle for simmering the sauce for the sloppy joes.

Another pain struck. She winced and stood motionless until it subsided.

Forgetting about the kettle she needed, she walked slowly to the living room to relax in her rocker with her cup of tea. She wouldn't let her brain think about what her body was warning her of right now. *I hope this goes away before my family comes over this evening. They worry about me enough as it is.*

A few minutes later, Meredith heard a knock on the door, and she slowly got up.

I wonder who that could be.

When she opened the door, she was surprised to see Jonah Miller standing on the porch. She hadn't seen him in several years, but he looked much as she remembered him from before — same curly black hair, dark brown eyes, and a small cleft in the middle of his chin. Except for being a little older, Jonah had hardly changed at all.

"Wie geht's?" Jonah asked, shifting from one foot to the other and leaning his hand on the door frame.

"Oh, Jonah, it's so good to see you." Meredith opened the door wider for him to enter. "I heard you were moving to Bird-in-Hand," she said, without answering his question.

Jonah gave a slow nod. "Got here yesterday, and I wanted to stop by and say how sorry I was to hear about your husband." He paused, and Meredith could see the sympathy he felt for her in his eyes. "If there's anything I can do for you, please let me know."

"Danki, I appreciate you coming over." Meredith really wasn't up to company right now, and she was about to say so, when another cramp came — this one much worse than the last. "Oh!" she gasped, doubling over from the pain. "I think I need to see a doctor right away."

With no hesitation, Jonah scooped Meredith into his arms and placed her on the sofa. Putting one of the small decorative pillows behind her head, he calmly told her, "I'm going out to the phone shack to call 911. Don't move or try to get up. Just lie here and rest. I'll be right back."

Trembling and fighting waves of nausea, Meredith drew in a deep breath and closed her eyes. *Dear Lord,* she silently prayed, rubbing her hand over her still-flat stomach, *please don't let me lose this baby. It's all I have left of Luke.*

ABOUT THE AUTHOR

New York Times bestselling author, **Wanda E. Brunstetter** became fascinated with the Amish way of life when she first visited her husband's Mennonite relatives living in Pennsylvania. Wanda and her husband, Richard, live in Washington State but take every opportunity to visit Amish settlements throughout the States, where they have several Amish friends. Wanda and her husband have two grown children and six grandchildren. In her spare time, Wanda enjoys photography, ventrilquism, gardening, beachcombing, stamping, and having fun with her family.

Visit Wanda's website at www.wanda brunstetter.com, and feel free to e-mail her at Wanda@wandabrun stetter.com.

The employees of Thorndike Press hope you have enjoyed this Large Print book. All our Thorndike, Wheeler, and Kennebec Large Print titles are designed for easy reading, and all our books are made to last. Other Thorndike Press Large Print books are available at your library, through selected bookstores, or directly from us.

For information about titles, please call:
(800) 223-1244

or visit our Web site at:
http://gale.cengage.com/thorndike

To share your comments, please write:
Publisher
Thorndike Press
10 Water St., Suite 310
Waterville, ME 04901

6-13.